MY FIRST HORSE

MY FIRST HORSE

By Will James

Mountain Press Publishing Company
Missoula, Montana
2004

First Printing, January 2004

Tumbleweed is a registered trademark of Mountain Press Publishing Company.

Library of Congress Cataloging-in-Publication Data

James, Will, 1892-1942.
  My first horse / Will James.
     p. cm.
Summary: A young cowboy describes his early experiences with horses, from a hobby horse
made of a cottonwood log to a horse-shaped pull-toy, and at last a real pony of his own.
  ISBN 0-87842-488-1 (cloth : alk. paper)
  [1. Horses—Fiction. 2. Cowboys—Fiction 3. Ranch life—Fiction.] I. Title.
  PZ7.J1545My 2003
  [Fic]—dc22

                                                   2003014814

PRINTED IN HONG KONG BY MANTEC PRODUCTION COMPANY

Mountain Press Publishing Company
Post Office Box 2399
Missoula, Montana 59806

≈ Publisher's Note ≈

WILL JAMES'S BOOKS are an American treasure. His writing and drawings captivated generations of readers with the lifestyle and spirit of the American cowboy and the West. Following James's death in 1942, the reputation of this remarkable writer and artist languished, and nearly all of his twenty-four books went out of print. But in recent years, publication of several biographies and film documentaries on James, public exhibitions of his art, and the formation of the Will James Society have renewed interest in his work.

Now, in conjunction with the Will James Art Company, Mountain Press is reprinting all Will James's books under the name the Tumbleweed Series, taking special care to keep each volume faithful to the original. Books in the Tumbleweed Series contain all the original artwork and text, feature an attractive new design, and are printed on acid-free paper.

The republication of Will James's books would not have been possible without the help and support of the many fans of Will James. Because all James's books and artwork remain under copyright protection, the Will James Art Company has been instrumental in providing the necessary permissions and furnishing artwork.

The Will James Society was formed in 1992 as a nonprofit organization dedicated to preserving the memory and works of Will James. The society is one of the primary catalysts behind a growing interest not only in Will James and his work, but also in the life and heritage of the working cowboy. For more information on the society, contact:

Will James Society • c/o Will James Art Company
2237 Rosewyn Lane • Billings, Montana 59102

Mountain Press is pleased to make Will James's books available again. Read and enjoy!

JOHN RIMEL

Books by Will James

MY FIRST HORSE

ALL MY LIFE I've liked horses better than anything else, and that's natural, for a cowboy has a lot to do with horses.

My first look-around when I came to earth was for horses and I wasn't disappointed for my dad had quite a few and I was in a country where there were many, and cattle too. But cattle didn't interest me. It was different with horses, for the sight of them always got me wanting to be near them and with them.

I've had plenty of horses of my own, one called Smoky and one called Big-Enough and another Scorpion, but the horse I'm going to tell about here was a different sort of a horse. It was my first one. And if you'd like to know what a cowboy does when he's very young, this will tell you.

When I was only a year old, my mother died and my father took me to live on a ranch where there was a woman to take care of me. I called her Mommy and I don't remember her husband's name so I'll just call him Tom. My Dad used to go off on long rides and leave me at the ranch.

There was a big ranch house made of logs, where I lived. Then some distance from the house were the corrals, fenced-in places where the horses and cattle were kept. I didn't know much about them when I first went there, I was too little. But just as soon as I was big enough I found my way down to the corrals where the horses were. And all my play was of horses, as I'll show you now.

One of the first things I remember well was a wooden horse on rockers. It was home-made all the way through, even to the rockers. The body was made from a cottonwood log and painted a blue-gray color. The mane and tail were of real horsehair, the ears of stiff leather. The saddle was an old pack saddle with the horns sawed off. It was covered with rawhide and odd pieces of leather so it looked near enough like a real one and it was light enough so I could put it back on the horse, even though the horse was taller than I was.

I had a great time saddling and unsaddling that horse, playing he was a sure-enough wild one like some of the real ones I saw down by the corrals. There was a rope on that saddle, too, and I played the old porch chairs were cattle. I'd manage to jerk one down once in awhile.

I remember that porch too, for that was the range where I rode my horse and did my bronco busting and steer roping. It was the whole length of the log house, wide, and made of rough cottonwood boards. I know they were rough boards because on that same porch I used to draw animals, mostly horses, with pieces of charcoal.

On account of Blue, which was the name I gave my wooden horse, I seldom left my territory, which was the big porch. If I could have moved Blue very far, I might have taken him down the path to the corrals to try to rope something else besides chairs and the cats. The wise ranch dog knew just how far I could throw my rope and never worried to budge much. But the few chickens that once in a while jumped up on the porch soon quit that. I never caught one, but the swish of the rope was enough to scare them away.

Noticing how I liked horses while I was so young, the people at the ranch gave me a surprise one winter I know I'll never forget. The weather was too cold and stormy for me to play outside much. So they figured on something for me to enjoy myself with while I was inside.

After returning from town one time they set up a small spruce tree in one corner of the main room, fixed it all up with candles and shiny, colorful ornaments. Then they told me to go to bed, saying I'd better stay there or Santa Claus wouldn't come. It was the first time I'd heard of Santa Claus, and I went to sleep wondering who he was and what it was all about.

When I woke up the next morning and came into the main room, I was told that all the packages around the lighted up tree were from Santa Claus, for me to play with.

I remember staring at the packages, not bothering what was in them at the time, for I'd spotted one little dappled-gray horse standing under the tree, and at the sight of him I forgot all else.

There's no saying how I enjoyed myself with that little gray horse most of that winter. He was too small to ride and there were no rockers under him, just a little flat board with wheels on it. But I could move him anywhere I wanted to and the shape of him was much better than Blue's, more like a real horse. His dappled-gray color was what struck me most, it was just like some of the real horses I'd seen being run into the corrals.

Among the other toys there was a little cart with harness, to go with the little gray. I'd rather have had a little saddle to fit him, one I could put on and cinch up as I did with Blue out on the porch. Blue even had a bridle which I would slip on and off, but with this little gray there was only a halter, glued on him and there to stay.

I hooked him to the cart a few times but he didn't look like a work horse to me. Even then it struck me as not right to put a good saddle horse into harness and I didn't care for it.

So with pieces of old boot tops, marlin spike and string I went to work trying to make a saddle for the little gray. I wasted one boot top and stuck my fingers a few times. Then Tom, the ranch owner, seeing what I was up to, came to my rescue and in a few evenings made me a little saddle. I made the hackamore myself with some cord. It didn't look at all like a hackamore but I could at least take it off and put it on. By that time I'd taken off all the glued-on supposed-to-be straps that were on the little gray. With the rigging that was slipped on him now he sure enough looked like a cow horse.

Then, as I went on playing with him, that little board on wheels under his feet got to bothering me, and long before spring came I had to take it off. Then he looked more like a real horse. I called him Thunder.

With the little gray horse to play with inside during bad weather and big Blue on the outside during good weather, I had a full time that winter .

When spring came, snows melted away and the ground dried in spots. I asked Tom to cut me some little willows about a foot in length. I wanted to build me corrals and a shed for my little gray. I would have cut them myself but there were none of the kind I wanted close enough to the house. The nearest were over a mile away. I got the corral "logs" in good time, enough to make a couple of good corrals and a shed. As the willows were green, I peeled them first so as to make neat corrals, like the big ones down below.

As soon as I had one corral made, the round one, I brought out the little gray, put him in it, unsaddled him and put the saddle to hang on the top "pole." It looked right natural.

Then I went on with the square corral and built a shed in one corner of it. When I finally got through, after many days, I figured I had a pretty neat spread. The only thing I needed was more stock. I got another glad surprise, for as the ranch owner went to town for his regular spring trip he took me along and I came back with two more little gray horses which I could use either as stock or saddle horses. I soon stripped them of their glued-on toy harness, took the little wheeled board out from under them, and for a spell I was right busy with the three, in and around my corrals. The big Blue on the porch was also brought down to have him near, but he was too big to fit in with the grays and he was sort of neglected.

When summer came I neglected my little grays some, too, for I'd got so I wanted to be near live horseflesh. So I was down by the big corrals whenever a bunch of horses or cattle was brought in. Sometimes a cowboy hoisted me on one of the gentle saddle horses and I'd sit in the big saddle watching all the cowboys were doing. And when my Dad came to visit me for a few days I'd ride out with him.

Early that fall a heavy rain came and, as it started, I put my three little grays under the "log" shed I'd built for them. I had to stay in the house during the storm but every once in a while I'd look at my ponies through the window. I felt satisfied that they were comfortable in their shelter. Blue was out in the weather, but he was big and tough and I figured it wouldn't hurt him.

The rain lasted away into the night, and next morning as it stopped and the skies were clear again, I went out to look at my "stock." Blue was all right, but it wasn't so well with the three grays, for the mud and sand had washed in on them and came up nearly to their hocks and knees.

I reached under the shed to pick up one of my little grays and I got a surprise and shock when he nearly slipped out of my hands. His papier-maché hide had been soaked during the rain and loosened from his body.

The roof of the little shed, made of dry grass with dirt on top, had leaked through during the heavy rain. Not only that, but it fell through, and the rain-soaked grass and dirt did a fine job of soaking my ponies' hides.

The first pony I "skinned" and placed his hide over the corral fence. That kind of made up for the loss of him because that hide sure looked natural spread out on the corral that way, the same as the beef and cow hides that were spread over the big square corral fence down below.

I aimed to be very careful with the other two and save them, if I could. So, instead of getting a hold of them by their side I raised them up from under the belly, as careful as if I'd been picking up a young humming bird. But that seemed to have even worse effect, for their wooden legs, stuck to the half dry washed-in mud, separated from their bodies. Their hides were also all soaked loose as a fallen leaf in the wind. Not thinking they might all be dried and glued back, I hung those hides over my corral fence, too.

I forget what I did with the "carcasses" but I must of lost interest in them. Anyhow I remember how them three gray hides looked so natural on my corral and how Tom had to laugh at the sight of them and tried to cheer me up for the loss of my stock, "even before winter come."

I went back to faithful old Blue then and had him put back on the big porch so he wouldn't also fall all to pieces. But I still had some enjoyment out of the remains of my three little grays, for every time I'd come near or pass by my little corrals I'd look at their hides a-hanging over them, looking so natural-like. Not so many years later I learned that a horse was too much thought of in our country to have his hide hanging on a corral fence. When one died it was left on him to go back to dust with.

Along with Blue I remember to've also done quite a bit of riding on real horses that fall, away late into the winter. The way I remember, it was my last fall and winter at that ranch. I used the same saddle on the live horses as I did on Blue, and with a blanket folded over it, it wasn't bad to ride in.

Now I was outside most every day, it seemed like no time before Christmas came again. Another tree was set up in the same corner of the main room and decorated up. When I was sent to bed that Christmas Eve and asked what I wanted Santa Claus to bring me I don't remember just what I said, but I know it had something to do with horses, maybe a real saddle and something for me to wear in it.

I had great faith in Santa Claus then, and I still have, but the ones I've known since didn't always come at Christmas time, it'd be most any time, and their looks and clothes weren't at all like the one I was shown pictures of. No one dressed as Santa for me then, either, but I was showed fresh cow tracks in the snow which I was told were his reindeer's tracks, the sled wasn't supposed to leave any tracks, and I believed all of that, for I wasn't disappointed when Christmas morning came.

I was sent to bed early that Christmas Eve, and it wasn't long afterwards when I heard voices of others coming into the house. There were hearty greetings and I thought some of the voices sounded familiar. It was mighty hard for me to take a peek, for the iron latch was heavy and it would sure make a noise if I tried to open the door. It was also hard for me to go to sleep for listening, but the voices finally quieted down. I didn't know any more that night.

Next morning I didn't wake until I felt my bed lifted and then dropped suddenly. There were greetings of "Merry Christmas," and, sitting up, I got the pleased and surprised sight of my grinning Dad at the foot of my bed. With him was Bopy, a friend of his.

That Christmas was the happiest and all around best I ever had. After all the first greetings were over and I was turned loose to the lit-up tree, I spotted two more little gray horses underneath the lower branches, then a rope, not of the kind that's got at toy shops but a light and hard-twist Mexican maguay. There were some packages too, but as before, I didn't pay much attention to them. But I was surprised when I was told to open them.— In one box was a pair of little copper-toed boots, the front half of the top red with a little white star in the center. I sure got all interested then and pounced on another box. In that one was a hat, the same kind my Dad wore only of my size, and inside of it was another package which contained what I still think was the finest little pair of spurs I've ever seen, not much silver on them, but they were hand-forged and with little star rowels.

All around, Santa Claus was mighty good to me. Of course, all the presents I got were from him, as I was told, the folks had only ordered them. But what I enjoyed most was having my Dad there for Christmas. He stayed until the next morning and then I was left to play to my heart's content.

I rode old Blue harder than ever for a while. When spring came I moved my corrals and shed to another location, a higher one and where no silt would wash in. I also made sure of a good roof on the shed this time. After that was all done I put my grays under the shed and the little saddle for them which I'd kept, hanging over the little corral. Old Blue, sort of scarred up, looking as if he needed a rest, was left on the porch and I went more and more to riding live horses again whenever I had the chance.

I had plenty of chances and got to make quite a nuisance of myself as the spring work started. I was down to the big corrals most every day and sometimes quite a few miles from them. A few times I caught some gentle horse by coaxing him into the barn with some grain, where by standing on the manger and stall I could bridle and saddle him and ride away for a spell by myself. I got caught at that too, but it was now too late and I'd about forgotten my two little grays and Blue.

Maybe for punishment for taking horses and riding away without permission, or maybe because everyone thought I'd outgrown my toy horses, it was quite a surprise and blow to me when one day as I came up to the house from the corrals I saw Blue standing on the porch, without his rockers under him. The rockers had been placed on a porch chair instead, one I used to rope at from Blue.

I remember well how I felt at the sight, it was as if his very hoofs had been sawed off, and, even though I hardly used him any more, he was my pet. I liked to see him there, resting from the long hard rides I'd given him, and still always ready to go some more, his old blue paint hide, play-scarred, worn to the wood and branded from ears to tail. Now with his action gone of a sudden, a cripple, he was worse to me than dead. He'd seemed near alive before and I'd sort of pensioned him, like a cowman would a good old cowhorse, before his day was done, and seeing his legs cut off was quite a bit too much for me.

The folks must have known how I felt, for old Blue disappeared from the porch. They must have known also that putting the old rockers back on him, or a new pair, wouldn't have done, for he wouldn't have been the same horse to me.

The rockers also disappeared from under the chair, and maybe to make up for it all I was given some live horse now and again and taken out riding more often, and nothing was said if I "stole" a horse and went riding by myself once in a while. I sort of took advantage of that.

But my grieving over the loss of Blue wasn't for so long. June came, and the day of my birth. I didn't know it was that day until night, when I got four wallops, and one to grow on. I sure didn't mind those wallops, for it was my Dad who had given them to me.

He'd ridden up that afternoon, leading what I thought was a pack horse. It was a little black horse, and as pretty a one as I'd ever seen. My Dad's bed was hitched on him and that looked good, for that meant he was to be with me for a time.

But the big surprise was still to come. At the right time, my Dad unhitched his bed and pulled it off the little black, and there, a-shining to the sun on the little black's back, was a brand new little saddle that fitted him perfectly.

I couldn't say a thing nor make a move at the sight but in the next few seconds I found that that little saddle fitted me too, for I was hoisted up into it and there I sat.

The way I felt, my eyes must have been as big as my heart right then, and while I was in that trance my Dad slipped a bridle on the little black's head.

I didn't come to until he handed me the reins and spoke.

"This outfit is all yours, Son," he says, "saddle, horse, and all."

I was four years old, on my very own first horse, and the whole world was mine.